For Ava and Scarlett

First published 2011 by Macmillan Children's Books
a division of Macmillan Publishers Limited
20 New Wharf Road, London N1 9RR
Basingstoke and Oxford
Associated companies throughout the world
www.panmacmillan.com

ISBN: 978-0-230-70107-6 (HB)
ISBN: 978-0-230-70383-4 (PB)

1 3 5 7 9 8 6 4 2

A CIP catalogue for this book is available from the British Library.
Printed in Belgium

JULIE MONKS

MARCELLO MOUSE
and the MASKED BALL

MACMILLAN CHILDREN'S BOOKS

Marcello Mouse lived alone in a dark hole, along a dark canal, in the darkest corner of Venice. But he longed for warmth, and he longed for music, and he longed for light.

The winter had been long,
the coldest Venice had ever known.
But with a twitch of his tiny nose,
Marcello could smell that spring was on
its way, and with spring came a magical event!

Marcello had spent the cold months preparing;
stitching and sewing, waiting and wondering.
At last, the special day arrived.

In the distance, Marcello Mouse
heard a beautiful song . . .

"One by one they come,
on the most magical night of all.
With a rustle of silk and a jingle of bells,
off to the magical ball."

With a squeak and a leap and
a flick of his tail, Marcello
slipped out of his door.
He hopped up
the steps . . .

over the
bridge . . .

. . . and along the canal, singing to himself as he scampered towards the twinkling lights in the distance.

With
each
mouse
step
the lights grew
brighter and the
music grew **louder.**

Marcello drew close to the Grand Palace . . .

. . . home of the Magical Masked Ball.

Marcello skipped lightly up the steps, smoothed
down his fur, and paused. For this little mouse
was **not** invited to the ball.

But as he stood in the doorway, his fur felt
warm and the air smelled sweet.

Quick as a flash
he slipped
inside!

How DARING!

How BOLD!

Marcello Mouse in a room full of

CATS!

But Marcello
was prepared.

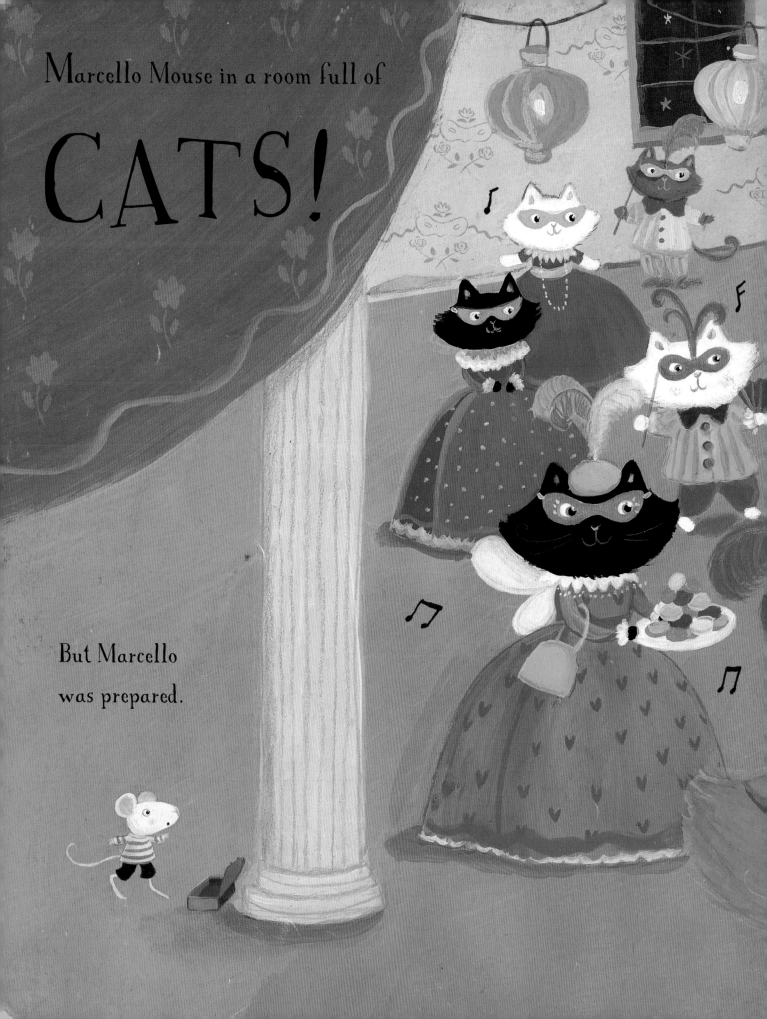

He had made a
cunning disguise!

They'll never guess,
thought Marcello
with a grin.

And with a leap of joy
he followed his nose
to a table full of food.

He tasted fine wine and wonderful cheese, and nibbled at cakes that were sugary sweet.

He was lively and funny and charming. *"What a nice fellow,"* the cats all agreed.

Then came the call,
"Let the dancing begin."
Light as a feather,
Marcello leaped to the floor . . .

. . . and began to DANCE.

He twisted
and turned,

he skipped
and he swung,

he tripped and
he twizzled,

then suddenly . . .

STOPPED!

Not a whisker twitched
and not a paw moved.

"That's no cat,
it's a MOUSE!"

Poor Marcello's tail began
to quiver in fright.
Then he let out a terrified . . .

"Squeak."

"I'll be Mice Cream by midnight!" cried Marcello,
dashing for the door. Swerving and skidding,
he shot across the floor.

He sped along the hallway and scampered down the steps.

He darted along the canal and tumbled over the bridge.

He ran without stopping and without looking back, until the bright lights of the ball were far behind him.

Back in his dark little mouse hole, Marcello shivered and trembled in fright.

"One by one they ran, on the most magical night of all. With a rustle of silk and a jingle of bells, away from the pussycat ball."

"I've been so silly," he sobbed. "They could have eaten me up!"

Slowly and sadly Marcello put his outfit away.

Then he curled up
into a little ball and
tried his hardest to
fall asleep.

All of a sudden,
there came a **loud knock!**

"CATS!"

Trembling, Marcello peered around the door.
But there on the mat, instead of a cat, was a
large, golden envelope.

And written on the envelope
was the name, *Marcello Mouse.*
"For me?" he squeaked.
"I've never had a letter."

The cats of Venice cordially invite brave Marcello Mouse, the amazing dancing mouse, to be guest of honour at the Summer Ball.

Marcello hopped and leaped for joy.
"They weren't going to eat me, they liked me!"
Marcello Mouse was a happy mouse once more.

And so, when the evening arrived,
a small, smartly dressed mouse left
his dark hole, along a dark canal,
in the darkest corner of Venice,
and made his way to the
grandest ball.

And there upon a sparkling stage,
Marcello Mouse, the amazing dancing mouse,
received the warmest welcome of all.